To: _____

From: _____

*For my wife, Louise, who told me about
the Little Reindeer.*

THE LITTLE REINDEER
A RED FOX BOOK 0099 456729

First published in Great Britain by Andersen Press Ltd 1996,

First Red Fox Mini Treasures edition published 2003

1 3 5 7 9 10 8 6 4 2

Copyright © Michael Foreman 1996

Red Fox Books are published by Random House Children's Books,
61-63 Uxbridge Road, London W5 5SA,
a division of The Random House Group Ltd,
in Australia by Random House Australia (Pty) Ltd,
20 Alfred Street, Milsons Point, Sydney, NSW 2061, Australia,
in New Zealand by Random House New Zealand Ltd,
18 Poland Road, Glenfield, Auckland 10, New Zealand,
and in South Africa by Random House (Pty) Ltd,
Endulini, 5A Jubilee Road, Parktown 2193, South Africa

THE RANDOM HOUSE GROUP Limited Reg. No. 954009

www.kidsatrandomhouse.co.uk

A CIP catalogue record for this book is available from the British Library.

Printed in China

The Little Reindeer

Michael Foreman

Mini Treasures

RED FOX

THE little reindeer wondered what all the fuss
was about.

He could see lights blazing in the windows of
the snow covered buildings. Shadowy figures rushed
in and out of doorways carrying mysterious bundles.

The little reindeer picked his way through
the deep snow towards the biggest building.
As he got closer he could hear singing and
banging, whirring and rustling.

The little reindeer peeped round the door into
the warm, noisy room.

Amazing animals were streaming between rows of singing people. The little reindeer moved further into the room and suddenly found himself being carried along amongst the rest of the animals.

He tried to back away but was pushed forwards by the animals pressing from behind. Suddenly they all disappeared in a blizzard of coloured paper.

He was turned over and over in swirling colours. Then it went black and cold and things bumped down on him until he couldn't move.

He heard jingling
bells and cheering and
he felt a great whoosh.

For hours they seemed to stop and start and swoop up and down until he was tumbling head over hoofs again.

He tried to move his legs, and managed to stand up. Although he was relieved to feel the softness of snow beneath his hoofs, he still couldn't see anything. The little reindeer stood in the darkness, surrounded by strange sounds. Then he heard footsteps crunching towards him.

Suddenly he found himself staring at an astonished face, and then a smile.

"Wow! What a present!" The boy picked him up and danced round and round in the snow.

"But where can I keep you? There are no pets allowed in the building. I know . . . You can stay up here with my pigeons,"

The boy opened the door of a large shed at one end of the roof. Immediately the sky filled with birds.

In a corner of
the shed the boy
made a straw bed
for the reindeer and
fetched milk and a whole
assortment of cereals.

"Tomorrow we can try lots of
different things to eat and see
which you like best."

Two by two the pigeons
returned to their perches.
They didn't seem to
mind the new visitor.

Each day the boy brought food and milk. The reindeer liked peanut butter sandwiches best of all. While the pigeons flew higher and higher in the sky, the boy and the reindeer strolled around the roof and watched the busy city life below.

The weather grew warmer and the little
reindeer grew bigger.

One day when the boy opened the door to let
the pigeons out, the reindeer flew
out with them.

The reindeer didn't fly far, that first time, just across to the neighbouring building and back. But as the days passed, he flew further and further.

The boy was overjoyed. He had told no one about his wonderful Christmas pet because he knew he would not be allowed to keep him.

By early summer the reindeer was big enough to give the boy rides around the roof on his back. Then, one evening, they flew together over the roofs of the city.

They flew together every night of the long summer and over the leaves of autumn.

When the first snowflakes of winter began to fall, the boy noticed a look of sadness in the reindeer's eyes. The boy hugged him as always, but the reindeer looked up at the swiftly moving grey clouds and sighed.

The boy knew that
only six or seven special
reindeer can fly every
generation. He even knew
their names.

He knew that his
reindeer was going to be
one of those very special
ones.

On Christmas Eve the boy gave the reindeer his favourite dinner and the pigeons sang. They were still singing when he kissed the reindeer goodnight.

From his bed, he thought he heard jingling bells, but he was probably dreaming by then.

Next morning he rushed up to the roof
but the reindeer had gone. There were
sleigh tracks in the snow. When he opened
the shed and all the pigeons flew out the
boy saw that each had a red ribbon collar
and a little jingle bell. In the reindeer's bed
of straw was a note -
"Dear Boy,
Thank you for looking after my
smallest reindeer.
See you next year.
Love,
Santa Claus."

Through the next spring, summer and autumn the boy heard the tinkling and jingling of bells each time the pigeons flew.

And on Christmas Eve, when he heard the real jingle bells coming down from the snowy sky, he was waiting on the roof with milk and peanut butter sandwiches.